❄ THE STARLIGHT SNOWDOGS ❄

THE LAND OF SNOW

*For Pat White, Arctic Expert
and Agent Extraordinaire*

First published in paperback by HarperCollins *Children's Books* in 2010

HarperCollins *Children's Books* is a division of HarperCollins *Publishers* Ltd,
77-85 Fulham Palace Road, Hammersmith, London W6 8JB.

Visit our website at: www.harpercollins.co.uk

1 3 5 7 9 10 8 6 4 2
ISBN: 978-0-00-735902-8

Text copyright © Julie Sykes 2010
Cover illustrations copyright © Andrew Farley 2010

Printed and bound in England by Clays Ltd, St Ives plc

THE STARLIGHT SNOWDOGS

THE LAND OF SNOW

Skye Waters

HarperCollins *Children's Books*

Chapter 1

Ella Edwards was only half listening to her friend Isabel Masters as they walked home. They'd been back at school for a week, but Ella wished it was still the holidays with long sunny days and no homework to spoil her fun. Ella craved adventure and the outdoors and hated being shut up in a stuffy classroom learning times tables and long multiplication.

"Mum said she'd buy me a DVD this weekend for helping her out with my brothers," said Isabel. "I might get the one about the talking cat who thinks he's a fireman. It's supposed to be really funny. The spy kids one looks good too."

Suddenly Ella heard a loud cry. She glanced at Isabel, but she was still chatting away about films.

There it was again. Ella looked around, mystified. The street was empty. Where could it be coming from?

"Ella, what's up?" Isabel suddenly realised that she had been talking to herself.

"That noise," said Ella. "It sounds like a dog howling."

"I can't hear it."

"It's really loud. It's coming from over there."

Ella headed down the street towards the entrance to the Country Park, where the howling seemed to be coming from.

"What's so special about a dog howling?" asked Isabel, running to catch her up. "You get loads of dogs barking in the park."

"This is different," Ella insisted. She hurried across the car park and turned right at the gate. The path stretched before her downhill, with thick bushes on one side and open grassland on the other. In the distance, a lady was throwing a stick for her dogs.

"Ella, we're supposed to go straight home," called Isabel.

"It's getting louder. You must be able to hear it now..." Ella ran down the path.

"I can't," insisted Isabel, reluctantly following her.

The howling was ear-splitting and Ella slowed, staring intently at the thick branches and leathery green leaves of the bushes. Was there a dog stuck inside? She leant forward, then jumped back in surprise as a large brown cardboard box suddenly skidded from under the bush in front of her and stopped at her feet. There was a pause as if the box was gathering energy, then it rocked from side to side, barking loudly. Sinking on to her knees,

Ella dropped her school bag on the floor and reached for the box, but Isabel got there first. Pushing in front of Ella she pulled open the cardboard lid, gasping in surprise at the cute black and white puppy squashed inside. Ella swallowed back her annoyance. She'd found the box, but now Isabel was taking over. That was so like her! Isabel didn't mean to be unkind, but she was a little bossy sometimes.

"Oh! You poor thing." Isabel gently grasped the puppy round its middle and lifted it out of the box.

"Yap!" The puppy wriggled free and jumped at Ella, licking her hands and face and making her giggle.

Gently, Ella scooped it up and the puppy

relaxed into her arms with a contented sigh.

For a moment, Isabel was taken aback. Her face clouded and she looked quite hurt, then, shaking her head, she laughed.

"She likes you best."

"He," said Ella, cradling the puppy close to her. She had a strong feeling that the puppy liked her best too, but not wanting to upset her friend she moved slightly so the puppy could see Isabel as well. "He likes you too. He's watching you."

The black and white puppy was soft and fluffy, with blue eyes, a long nose and enormous fox-like ears that were too big for his body. Fastened round his neck was a blue collar with a dog tag in the shape of a shiny silver snowflake dangling from it. Ella reached for the snowflake, thinking it might have the dog's name and the owner's telephone number engraved on it. But instead of writing, the tag was etched with miniature patterns, just like a real snowflake. It felt icy cold and as Ella touched it the snowflake seemed to spark with tiny electrical pulses that made her fingers tingle. Suddenly the puppy looked right at her. His eyes were the brightest blue she'd ever seen. Impulsively she held him closer, loving the feel of his silky fur and his gorgeous puppy smell.

"That's pretty," said Isabel, reaching out to touch the dog tag and squealing with delight when the puppy licked her finger.

Ella stroked the puppy's soft neck.

"He's so cute. How could anyone leave him in a box?"

"What are we going to do with him?" asked Isabel anxiously. "We can't leave him here, but Mum will have a fit if I take him home. I'm not allowed pets. Mum says she's busy enough looking after Billy, Jack and me."

"I'll have him," blurted out Ella. She wanted the puppy more than anything else in the world.

"Will your mum let you?" Isabel sounded doubtful.

"She might," said Ella. "She's in all day and we've got other pets."

Mrs Edwards ran an internet business

selling greetings cards and worked from home, in a room she called her office. The family had an elderly cat called Spooks and four silky bantams — small fluffy hens that reminded Ella of teddy bears.

Cradling the puppy in the crook of her arm, Ella stood up. The puppy wriggled himself into a more comfortable position, then thumped his tail approvingly. Ella kissed the top of his head and the puppy licked her arm.

"I'll carry your bag," offered Isabel, picking it up.

"Thanks. Can you manage the box too? We shouldn't leave it here to litter the park."

Isabel flattened the box by standing on it so that it was easier to carry, then pushed it into

a bin as they walked past. Ella looked around her, nervously scanning the area. What if someone tried to claim the puppy back? She hugged the puppy tighter, overwhelmingly desperate to keep him. The puppy had been abandoned, she reassured herself. Why else had he been left in a box under a bush?

It took them ages to get home. The puppy had fallen asleep in Ella's arms, so they had to walk very slowly so as not to disturb him. Isabel didn't complain once, even though she had the boring job of carrying their school bags. Despite Isabel sometimes being a bit bossy, Ella knew she was lucky to have such a good friend.

Mum was watching from her office

window and opened the front door before Ella could get her key out.

"You're late. I was beginning to worry—" she broke off, suddenly noticing the sleeping puppy. "Oh, how cute! Where did it come from?"

"He's been abandoned," said Ella. "Someone left him in a cardboard box in the Country Park."

"Ella! What were you doing in the park? You're supposed to come straight home."

"I heard the puppy barking," said Ella. "He sounded upset. It's a good job we found him. He's far too small to be out on his own. Can I keep him? Please, Mum?"

Ella had often asked if she could have

a dog, but this time was different. She felt strangely drawn to the cuddly puppy sleepily snuffling in her arms. She couldn't explain it, but Ella knew they were meant to be together.

"He's very sweet." Mum hesitated. "Come indoors while I think about it."

"Please," Ella wheedled. "I've always wanted a dog and this one's special. Look how gorgeous he is."

"I don't know, Ella," said Mum. "It's a big decision. I'll have to talk to your dad about it first. He likes dogs, but he's not keen on having one, in case it messes up his garden."

At least Mum hadn't said no. Now all Ella needed to do was to persuade Dad to let the puppy stay. She was sure that once

Dad got to see him he'd agree.

"Thanks, Mum." If her arms hadn't been full of puppy, Ella would have hugged her.

"Come on, Izzy. Let's make the puppy a bed and find him something to eat."

Isabel looked at her watch and pulled a sad face.

"I wish I could, but I promised Mum I'd help her with Billy and Jack. They're such a handful." Gently she stroked the puppy's head. "What'll you call him if your dad says you can keep him?"

"Blue."

Ella glanced at the puppy. The name had come out before she'd even thought about it, but immediately she knew it was right.

"Blue," said Isabel, trying it out. "Like his eyes."

"Blue looks like a type of husky dog," said Ella's mum thoughtfully. "Did you know they come from the Arctic?"

"A husky!" exclaimed Ella. "Wow!"

The snowflake on Blue's collar seemed to sparkle more brightly. Ella couldn't resist touching it, and there it was again. That feeling, like the snowflake was sparking with a strange sort of energy that made her fingers fizz. She closed her eyes and immediately saw a picture of six husky dogs pulling a sled across a snowy landscape. It was so real, Ella imagined herself riding with them, an Arctic wind whipping across her face, snow freezing on her eyelashes.

"Ella? I said, ring me when your dad gets in."

Isabel pulled on Ella's arm, tugging her out of her daydream. Shivers fizzled up and down her spine. That was amazing! Ella loved the magical white world with the sled pulled by snowdogs.

"I'll ring you," she agreed, going to the door with her friend.

As Ella went indoors, Blue began to stir. Yawning daintily, he opened his eyes and stared up at her. His look was so intense it felt as if he were begging Ella to let him stay. But her dad was a keen gardener and every year his vegetables won prizes at the county show.

Would Ella really be allowed to keep Blue?

"I'll find a way," she whispered. "I promise."

Chapter 2

Ella had homework and knew she should start it. Getting it done would work in her favour when she asked Dad about keeping Blue. She dragged her school bag over to the kitchen table and pulled out her exercise book and pencil case. It was maths tonight. Ella grumbled under her breath as she read through the questions. Hadn't she worked hard enough at school? Blue gave a small bark.

"I know," said Ella. "I'd much rather be playing with you too."

Blue climbed out of the cardboard-box bed Ella had made him earlier, pricking up his ears as if he was listening to something. He barked again, louder this time.

"Blue, quiet."

"Wooo!" Throwing back his head, Blue howled and ran to the door.

"Ssssh," said Ella. "Mum's still working."

"Woof!" Blue's bark was surprisingly deep for a puppy as he frantically scratched at the door.

Ella jumped up. Blue's howls really were too insistent to be ignored.

"Oh! Do you need to go out? Clever boy!"

As soon as Ella opened the door, Blue raced outside. She followed, expecting him to stop on the grass, but instead Blue shot down the garden as if he was on an urgent mission. The silky bantams scattered, squawking indignantly, and Spooks quickly climbed on to the shed, moving much faster than he normally did.

"Blue, wait!"

Ella chased after him, past Dad's vegetable patch and on towards her den, an old brightly painted caravan at the bottom of the garden. Thinking the puppy would stop when he reached the fence, Ella slowed up. But Blue was getting faster.

"Blue, stop!"

Ella grew even more alarmed as Blue continued running towards the fence. He was going to hurt himself. Determined to stop him, she leapt forward, throwing herself at the dog and catching him round his tummy. With incredible strength Blue kept going, pulling Ella over and dragging her across the ground. Elbows and knees grazing the earth, Ella gritted her teeth and hung on tight. In the distance she was sure she could hear dogs howling. Blue seemed to answer them, his voice sounding urgent. The fence loomed closer and Ella closed her eyes, bracing herself for the crash. Suddenly her stomach dipped as if she were riding in a lift, cold air rushed at

her face and her hair streamed out behind her in light brown ribbons. Opening her eyes, Ella gripped Blue in disbelief. They were flying! Ella stared at the houses and gardens growing smaller and smaller beneath her, until everything was so tiny it was like looking down at a map.

The light was fading and the sky darkened, blotting out the shrinking landscape, as the air turned bitterly cold. Ella shivered, bewildered by the pitch-black sky. It was impossible to see where she was going. What was happening?

She clutched Blue tighter as the rushing wind continued to hit her in the face. It was hard to breathe and impossible to call out for

help. Ella wasn't even sure which way up they were!

There was snow in the air. It swirled around Ella, engulfing her in an icy white sheet and wrenching Blue from her frozen fingers.

"No!" Ella screamed.

There was nothing she could do to save Blue. She couldn't even save herself. The snowstorm was too sudden and too violent, tossing her around like a sock in a tumble dryer. The wind stung her eyes, making them water and freezing the tears as they ran down her cheeks. Ella screwed up her eyes and wrapped her arms round her body. She was terrified of falling out of the sky and felt awful for letting go of Blue. The blizzard threw Ella around until she wondered how much longer she could last without fainting from the cold.

Then at last the storm began to calm. Ella opened her eyes and stared around in amazement. She was flying across an inky sky spangled with stars! It was so beautiful. Ella stopped gazing around when she realised her fingers were numb from gripping something. Looking down, she was startled to find that she was riding on a wooden sled, pulled by a small husky dog. *This has to be a dream*, thought Ella. But it felt too real to be a dream. As Ella flexed her numb fingers, she suddenly realised she was wearing gloves. Where had they come from? She hadn't been wearing gloves when she was doing her homework. She didn't recognise the thick red jacket with the fur-trimmed hood she had on either. Ella saw she was also wearing matching padded trousers and a pair of sturdy boots. She wriggled her toes, noticing how warm her feet felt in an extra cosy pair of socks. And she was wearing snow glasses! Ella touched them with her gloved hand. What was happening?

The sled flew on and Ella stopped wondering about the clothes and got swept up in the ride. It was so fantastic, she wanted to remember it all. She was surprised when the husky suddenly dived downwards. Ella gripped the sides of the sled, breathless with fear as they plummeted through the sky.

Were they going to crash?

Mysterious green lights danced around Ella, pulsating and twirling in long strands that stretched across the whole sky. *What are they?* She held out her arms in wonder as her body glowed green. She was so absorbed by green flashes and sparkling starlight that made her skin tingle like magic, Ella forgot that she was soaring downwards. With a rude jolt she hit the ground, a flash of green light illuminating her one final time. The sled upturned, tipping Ella face down in a snowdrift. Too stunned to move, she lay where she'd fallen.

Everything hurt, but the snow was soft and welcoming, soothing her aches and bruises. Ella sank further into it and relaxed, until someone tugged her arm.

"Urrrr," she groaned.

The tugging grew stronger and was accompanied by yaps and growls. Then a voice nearby said, "You have to get up. Hurry or you'll freeze."

"I can't," Ella answered.

"Please try." The voice was insistent and couldn't be ignored. Clumsily, Ella scrambled to her feet. The darkness had gone and in its place was a snowy landscape dotted with trees that stretched for miles. Ella looked around, wondering who'd found her, but she was alone except for a husky. The dog crouched down, resting his nose on his paws as if bowing to Ella.

"Did you hurt yourself?"

Ella glanced behind again, even though she knew there was no one there.

"I'm sorry about the bumpy landing. It was my first time."

The husky cocked his head, fixing Ella with its big blue eyes. Ella stared back uncertainly. Surely that wasn't the dog talking to her? Her eyes widened with surprise when she realised it was!

"I don't understand. Who are you?" she asked, self-consciously.

"It's me, Blue."

The husky crept forward and nudged Ella's gloved hand with his nose. Although he was still a young dog, he seemed larger than her

puppy Blue.

"The magic here makes me bigger and stronger," said the husky.

"Magic!" Ella felt a thrill of excitement. She'd always believed in magic, even when people told her that it was only make-believe.

Ella studied the dog closely. He did look like Blue. He had exactly the same markings and a glittering silver snowflake dog tag hung from his collar. Ella felt drawn towards it. Even through her gloves she felt a bubbling feeling in her fingers as she touched it.

Blue nuzzled her with his nose. Ella stroked his head, rubbing him faster as Blue butted her hand with approval. There were so many things she wanted to ask that she didn't know where to start.

Then from behind her came the sound of animals panting. Ella spun round as she saw four magnificent husky dogs and one smaller one running towards her. Ella's body tensed, unsure whether to stay where she was or move out of the way as the dogs sped closer. Effortlessly they pounded across the landscape, weaving their way between snow-laden trees, leaping over tiny humps. Running into a dip they disappeared momentarily. As they came over the top, Blue dropped to his belly, his nose resting in a patch of long coarse grass poking through the snow. The lead dog raced past him, stopping at Ella's feet.

"Hello." The dog's voice was low and

commanding, even though his mouth never moved. "The Starlight Snowdogs welcome you to the Arctic."

Chapter 3

The dog's leader was a handsome animal with a white face, brown eyes and a broad black head. One paw's step behind him stood a slightly smaller dog with orangey brown markings and big brown eyes.

"I'm Acer, this is my sister, Honey," Acer said as he indicated the orangey brown dog. "That's Bandit and Coda. Then there's Inca and her brother, Blue, who you already know. Inca and Blue are trainees; they've only just joined the Starlight Snowdogs team."

"Hello," said Ella eagerly, wanting to stroke them, but not sure if she should.

Honey stepped forward and pushed her nose into Ella's hand. Bandit was next, followed by Coda and Inca. When the introductions were finished, Acer stood in front of Ella.

"The Starlight Snowdogs need a new leader." He paused, before continuing. "And you have been chosen for that role. It is a very special honour that I hope you will want to accept. As our leader, you will be expected to help the animals that live here in our snowy land."

"What sort of help?" asked Ella shyly.

Thankfully Acer was quick to explain. "The world is changing. Progress can be a good thing, but sometimes it damages environments and harms the animals that live in them. As our leader, you will be expected to solve any harmful problems in the land of snow."

"That sounds hard," said Ella.

"It won't be easy. But if you agree to the role, you'll find strengths hidden inside that will help you carry out your duties."

Ella was intrigued. She was good at lots of things, but only because she worked hard and didn't give up easily.

"What sort of strengths?" she asked curiously.

"You will have to discover that for yourself." Acer's brown eyes were serious.

Ella hesitated. She desperately wanted to say that she'd help the Starlight Snowdogs to look after the Arctic, but was she really good enough to be their leader?

"Trust me," said Acer softly. "You can do this, as long as you believe in yourself. Please, climb on to the sled and we'll take you on a ride over our snowy land. When you see how wild and beautiful it is – and how magical – it may help you to decide."

"Thank you," said Ella. "I'd like that."

The sled was lying on its side and she tugged it with both hands, trying to free it from the snow.

"Think strong," urged Acer, his voice low and clear.

Ella glanced at him. Was he teasing her? Acer nodded encouragingly and at once Ella knew this wasn't a joke. Gripping the sledge tightly, she imagined she was exceedingly strong. She pulled again and as she concentrated, the muscles in her arms prickled and tensed. Gradually the sled became lighter until suddenly it was free and she was able to right it. She stared at it delightedly. How had she done that?

"Well done," said Acer, pawing the snow.

Ella beamed and climbed aboard, leaning comfortably against the sled's back rest. The Starlight Snowdogs took up their places in the harness: Acer and Honey in the lead, followed by Blue and Inca, with Bandit and Coda at the back.

Ella went to take the reins, then hesitated. She'd never driven a sled in her life. What was she supposed to do?

"Just hold them for now," said Acer. "You can learn how to drive next time."

Shivers of excitement ran up Ella's spine as she picked up the reins. The dogs took off across the snow, running so fast that it took Ella's breath away. The scenery flashed past, leaving her with mixed-up images of a vast landscape covered in snow. There were hills and valleys, thick green forests and a wide river, slushy with ice. Ella had never been to such a wild place, empty of all the clutter of modern living, where animals were free to roam. It was exhilarating and frightening at the same time.

Entranced, Ella leant forward, squeaking with delight when she saw polar bears lumbering along on all fours, snow-white Arctic foxes, caribou and lean wolves that hid amongst the snow-flecked trees as she passed. The dogs climbed a hill and Ella held on tight as the sled bounced and bumped to the top, then down the other side. The air was so fresh it made her lungs tingle and as the land flattened, Ella was delighted to find there was a beach at the bottom of the hill.

As the dogs raced alongside the half-frozen

sea, Ella stared in amazement at the seals and walruses, swimming in the icy water. These were animals Ella had only seen in books or on television. She wished the Starlight Snowdogs would slow down so she could look for longer, but they raced on until finally they approached the outskirts of a small town.

It was very different from the towns Ella was used to. It was much less crowded and the houses looked too fragile to withstand the harsh conditions. Passing by a long salmon-coloured house with a pointed roof, the dogs slowed to a jog. An elderly Inuit woman with a weather-beaten face and a young boy about Ella's age were standing at a window. The woman smiled and raised her hand. Ella stared in surprise, then, remembering her manners, she waved back. The woman's smile broadened, but the boy turned away. For a moment, his expression troubled Ella and she wondered why he looked so sad. But the dogs ran on, the town blurred, and soon they were back in the snowy landscape. Ella was impressed by how much stamina the dogs had, and also their incredible sense of direction.

At last the dogs pulled up. Half recognising a patch of long grass poking through the snow, Ella thought they might be back where they'd started. The six dogs stood there with ears pricked forward, sides heaving and steam coming from their panting mouths. After a long silence Acer spoke. "Whenever we pull the sled on land, we need the command to go free."

"Oh!" Ella blushed. "Sorry! Of course you can go free."

At once the harnesses fell away and the dogs rolled in the snow. Blue was playfully waving his paws in the air, flashing his white tummy as he rolled on his back.

After a little rest, Acer called everyone to order with a sharp bark. Honey stood by his side and when Bandit tried to edge her out, Acer gave a low growl. Bandit stopped pushing Honey and stepped back.

"That was fantastic. Thank you," said Ella, addressing Acer.

"So," he answered, thoughtfully pawing a

groove in the snow. "Will you help us? Do you accept the challenge of leading the Starlight Snowdogs?"

Images of the snow-covered land and the animals that lived there flashed through Ella's mind. It was the most wonderful place she'd ever visited. Ella knew she must do everything she could to help it stay that way. Suddenly she was aware of six pairs of eyes watching her. Looking up, she saw that Blue's were the keenest. Ella smiled at him and he ever so slightly cocked his head in return.

"Yes, please," said Ella, beaming. Then she added eagerly, "What do I have to do first?"

Acer barked his approval, and the other dogs joined in until he silenced them with a growl. Pushing his nose into Ella's gloved hand, Acer said, "That's enough for today. The Starlight Snowdogs will howl when we need you next. Blue will hear them and he'll transport you here. Blue and his magic snowflake collar are your links to us."

Reaching out, Ella stroked Blue's dark head. So she'd been right! There was a special bond between her and the dog. But why had she, Ella Edwards, been chosen to be their new leader when she lived thousands of miles away from their land? There were so many questions Ella wanted to ask.

Acer's voice cut gently into her thoughts. "It's time to go home," he said.

Ella sighed, the questions would have to

wait. Blue was already in place in the harness. Remembering her terrifying yet strangely wonderful journey to the Arctic, Ella gripped the sled's sides as Blue began to run across the snow. Acer, Honey, Bandit, Coda and Inca ran alongside, howling and waving their tails. Ella's stomach dipped as Blue jumped into the air, pulling the sled with him.

"Goodbye," she called quickly, then closed her mouth against the freezing air. A flash of green lit up the sky, then everything went dark. Ella held on tightly, but the ride was smoother than before. There was no snowstorm and no magical starlight, just black air swirling around the sled as Ella travelled home.

"Ready to go down?" Blue's voice rang out clearly and Ella nodded, then shouted back, "Yes."

As Blue dropped towards the ground, Ella braced herself for the crash. Seconds later, they landed with a small bump. Ella fell on her feet, narrowly missing her dad's compost pile and she giggled with relief. She looked around for the sled, but it had disappeared. Blue was skidding to a halt by her den at the bottom of the garden. Ella blinked. It was almost as if she'd never been away and was still chasing the puppy down the garden. But she knew that the starlight adventure had been real. Scooping Blue into her arms, she held the puppy up to her face. "Thank you. That was brilliant fun."

"Yap!" barked Blue, licking her nose.

"Yuk!" Chuckling, Ella carried the puppy indoors, running the last few paces as she saw through the kitchen window that Dad was home.

"Hello, Ella what happened to your homework?" he asked as she bounded indoors.

"Blue happened."

Thrusting the puppy forward, Ella began talking at double speed.

"Slow down," said Dad, as she explained how she'd found Blue.

"So can I keep him?" Ella finished.

Mr Edwards frowned and, using his reasonable voice, said, "You can't keep him without trying to find out where he's come from. Huskies are valuable dogs. People pay a lot of money for them."

"Not Blue," Ella insisted. "We found him in a cardboard box. He's been abandoned."

Mr Edwards raised his eyebrows as Blue attacked the leg of the kitchen table.

"Down!" he said firmly, pushing the eager puppy away.

"Please, Dad. You know how much I want a dog. I promise I'll look after him. He won't be any trouble."

"He is trouble already." Dad pulled his foot back as Blue began attacking his slipper. The puppy pounced on her dad's foot then slid off, landing on his back in a heap of waving legs and wrinkled tummy. Ella burst out laughing and even her dad chuckled too. Then suddenly he became serious.

"I don't know, Ella. A dog is a huge responsibility. And what if Blue ruins the garden?"

"He won't!" said Ella firmly.

Dad stared out of the window and Ella held her breath. How could she lead the Starlight Snowdogs if he sent Blue away?

Her dad smiled. "You're just like Grandad Edwards. He's mad about dogs too. He's had several over the years. You should email him, Ella. He'd love to hear about Blue."

Grandad Edwards lived in Canada. He didn't visit very often because of his dogs – three black Labradors – but he was always emailing.

"That's a good idea," said Ella. "Can I send him a photo too?"

Her dad nodded.

"He'd like that. Now don't get too excited. I'll check with the park warden to see if anyone's reported a missing puppy. If Blue isn't claimed, then you can keep him on trial. But it'll be up to you to look after him. That means feeding, walking and clearing up any mess he makes. And training too — Blue has to learn how to fit in with us and behave."

"Thanks, Dad," Ella's breath huffed out in relief. Looking after Blue would be easy. Being leader of the Starlight Snowdogs would be the difficult part! Ella bent down and stroked Blue's soft head. Her fingers caught on the silver snowflake and it made them fizzle. Ella shivered with excitement. She recognised that feeling now. It was magic! She couldn't wait to return to the Arctic to help the animals there.

"You'll be a good dog, won't you, Blue?"

"Yap," agreed Blue, thumping his tail on Ella's foot.

Chapter 4

As Ella was finishing her homework, her big sister Daisy came in from ice-skating practice. She was amazed to see Blue.

"He's so sweet," she cooed, tickling him under the chin. "I can't believe Dad said you can keep him."

"He's on trial," said Ella.

"You'd better be good then, Blue," said

Daisy. "You're too gorgeous to be sent away."

Ella spent the rest of the evening playing with her puppy. He had tons of energy. She took him into the garden with an old ball and tried to get him to play fetch, but Blue wasn't very good at it.

"Blue, drop!" giggled Ella, chasing him round the garden.

"When I throw the ball you're supposed to catch it and bring it back, not run off with it."

Ella gave up on trying to play catch and stood still with her hands behind her back. When Blue realised he wasn't being chased, he sat and stared at Ella, his triangular ears pointing upwards.

"You're so cute," she told him.

Blue thumped his tail in reply. It was black with a white tip that made it look like it had been dipped in paint. He had a rich black coat and white fur on his pink tummy. His legs were black to the knees and his paws, chest and face were whiter than the Arctic! He had a white mark on his forehead in exactly the shape of a snowflake.

"Give me the ball, Blue," said Ella, taking one step forward.

Blue tossed the ball in the air and gambolled after it, his bottom wiggling as he ran. Ella dived to the left, lunging forward to snatch the ball from him, but Blue suddenly changed direction and pranced away.

"Blue! You cheeky boy, give me the ball,"

giggled Ella, running after him again.

"That's not the way to give a dog a command," said Dad, coming down the garden towards Ella. "Dogs are very intelligent, but they can't understand whole sentences. You have to give them simple commands."

Her dad stood still and called out, "Blue, come."

Blue's ears twitched, but he kept running.

"Blue, come," said Dad firmly.

Blue hesitated, then changing direction, he bounded towards her dad.

"Good boy," said Dad, praising him in a sing-song voice. He bent down and patted Blue, repeating, "Good boy."

Then Ella's dad stopped petting Blue and said clearly, "Blue, drop."

Blue cocked his head on one side as if he didn't understand.

"Drop," said Dad, gently tugging the ball.

Blue tugged back, but Ella's dad refused to be drawn into a tug-of-war. Pointing at the ball, he repeated sternly, "Drop."

Meekly Blue dropped the ball at his feet.

"Good boy," said her dad, patting him again.

Ella was amazed. "Where did you learn how to do that?" she asked.

"From your grandad, Ella. He felt it was important for the whole family to know how to treat his dogs. He taught Granny, me and your Aunty Claire all the right commands. You have to let a dog know exactly who's in charge or it will always get the better of you. If Blue stays, we'll sign you both up for puppy-training classes, when he's old enough. Grandad always took his puppies to be trained."

Ella felt suddenly wobbly inside. She'd almost forgotten Blue was on trial. She'd have to take his training seriously or Blue's playful nature could get him into trouble. Taking a few steps away from Dad she called, "Blue, come."

"Yap!" barked Blue, springing into the air. He trotted towards Ella, then suddenly veered away, playfully wagging his tail.

He looked so sweet Ella badly wanted to chase after him, but she knew she mustn't. It wasn't right to play when she'd given him a command.

"Make your voice lower and say it like you really mean it," said her dad helpfully.

Swallowing back her frustration, Ella said in a clear low voice, "Blue, come."

At once Blue came towards her and stood so close one of his paws was on her foot.

"Good boy," smiled Ella.

"Well done," said her dad. "Now give him lots of praise."

That was easy! Ella patted Blue's soft fur, giggling as he licked her in return.

Ella's dad pulled his mobile phone out of

his pocket and took a photo of Blue, then one of Blue and Ella together to send to Grandad Edwards.

"Can we send them to Grandad now?" asked Ella, scooping a wriggly Blue into her arms.

"When I've watered my vegetables and shut the bantams in their hutch for the night," said her dad. "Go in and switch the computer on."

Ella carried Blue indoors, holding him close so his soft fur brushed her face, breathing in his biscuity smell. She put him down on the towel inside his makeshift cardboard-box bed.

"Night, Blue. Sleep tight," said Ella, gently

stroking along his white nose to the top of his black head.

Blue grunted contentedly, then snuggled down in his box with his tail curled round his body and his eyes closed. Unable to take her eyes off him, she backed out of the kitchen.

Ella was so happy she felt she might burst, but she was also tired after her exciting day. After sending an email with the photos of Blue to Grandad Edwards, Ella had a quick shower then went to bed, falling asleep immediately.

A few hours later, a high-pitched cry woke her. Struggling to open her eyes, Ella reached for the bedside light and switched it on. What was that awful noise? It sounded like... Blue!

Pushing back the duvet, Ella leapt out of bed, then shoved her feet into slippers whilst reaching for her dressing gown hanging on the back of the door. Ella had to stop Blue before his cries woke everyone else. Suddenly Ella's skin prickled with goose bumps. Did the Starlight Snowdogs need her? Ella caught her breath with excitement. She was longing to go back to the Arctic, but hadn't thought that it would happen again so soon. Ella wrenched open her wardrobe and grabbed her long woolly scarf and a winter coat. Using the light spilling from her open bedroom door to guide her, she crept downstairs. Blue's howls were getting more frantic as Ella opened the kitchen door. He was out of the cardboard-box bed with his nose pressed against the back door.

"Sssh," she whispered, hurrying towards him.

Quickly Ella took the back-door key from its hook and opened the door. Her hands were trembling and her stomach fluttering with a mixture of excitement and nerves. As soon as the door had been opened, Blue disappeared into the garden, his white paws flashing in the dark as he galloped across the grass.

"Wait," hissed Ella urgently. Still wearing slippers, she chased after him. "Blue, wait for me."

A slim crescent moon lit up the garden.

Ella stumbled after Blue, the cool night air brushing her face. When Blue had first transported her to the Arctic, Ella had been touching him. She strongly suspected that that was how the magic worked. But what if she couldn't catch him this time? Would he go without her? She hurtled on, her feet slipping in the dewy grass.

"Blue, wait," called Ella. She lunged forward and caught him by his collar, closing her eyes and bracing herself to be swept up into the air. To her surprise, however, Blue jolted to a halt. Ella's feet slid from under her and she landed on her bottom. Crouching down, Blue did a long wee then scraped the ground with his back paws.

Ella's face crumpled with disappointment. There was no flying sled ride, no magical starlit sky or mysterious flashing green lights. No Starlight Snowdogs waiting to transport her round the ice-cold Arctic landscape...

Then Ella realised she was on her own in the dark garden. Blue was trotting back into the house, his bottom waggling as he jumped up the step to the patio. She groaned as she noticed that someone had turned the kitchen light on. Now there'd be trouble. She ran after Blue, then scooped him up, hugging him against her chest as she went indoors.

Ella's mum stood in the kitchen, dressed in her long white dressing gown with her wavy blonde hair sticking up, looking sleepy and puzzled.

"Ella, what's going on? Were you going somewhere?" she asked.

"Blue needed the toilet," said Ella. "He could have made a puddle in the kitchen, but he didn't. He was very clever and woke me up instead."

"Oh! Well, I'm glad Blue didn't make a mess." Her mum yawned. "I hope he's not going to make a habit of this, though. I've got a big card order to get out tomorrow."

"What's all the noise about?" Daisy shuffled into the kitchen, her eyes widening as she saw Ella. "What are you doing? Are you running away?"

"I was taking Blue to the toilet," said Ella defensively.

"Dressed like that? It's September, not mid-winter!" said Daisy.

Ella's face burned with embarrassment.

"Anyway, I'm going back to bed," said Daisy. "I've got a long day tomorrow. Flute practice at lunchtime, then ice skating after school."

Daisy skated for a club and was very good. She'd won lots of big competitions.

"Me too," said their mum, following Daisy out of the kitchen. "Don't forget to switch off the light, Ella, and be quick. Put Blue back in his bed, then go back to yours."

"I will," said Ella.

She carried Blue over to his cardboard box

and carefully put him down, giggling as he licked her nose. Ella reached out and caught Blue's silver snowflake dog tag in her hand. The blue collar sparkled like starlight and the snowflake tingled against her skin with tiny electric pulses. Ella's earlier disappointment faded. The Starlight Snowdogs would tell her when she was needed meanwhile, she had Blue to look after.

Grinning to herself, Ella shrugged off her coat. Then she remembered the magical clothing she'd suddenly found herself wearing on her trip to the Arctic, and realised that she didn't need to dress up warmly anyway.

"I've got lots to learn, haven't I?" she whispered to Blue.

Blue thumped his tail, as if agreeing with her.

Ella gave him one last stroke, then after switching off the light, she went back upstairs to bed.

Chapter 5

Very early the next morning, Isabel arrived. Dumping her school bag on the hall floor, she thrust a carrier bag at Ella.

"I got it at the pet shop," she said, as Ella pulled several tins of puppy food out of the bag.

"Thanks, Isabel," said Ella gratefully. "This is brilliant. Blue had to have scrambled eggs last night and cereal mixed with water this morning. Dad says he needs three meals a day while he's still a puppy. He can have proper puppy food for lunch now."

"You're a life-saver," agreed Mrs Edwards. "I can't really spare the time to go shopping for Blue today. I've added dog food to my online shop, but that's not coming until tomorrow. Isabel, how much do we owe you?"

Isabel shook her head. "It's a present," she said firmly. "Where's Blue?"

"He's in the kitchen," said Ella, leading the way.

"I'm starting work now, so shut Blue in the kitchen when you go to school," called her mum.

Blue was very pleased to see Isabel and threw himself at her legs, barking loudly.

"He remembers me!" said Isabel, squatting down to pet him. "Ooh! That tickles. Stop licking me! I've already washed my face this morning."

Ella felt a sudden flash of jealousy that Blue was making such a fuss of Isabel, then quickly felt ashamed. She and Blue had a special bond that Isabel could never share. As the girls were leaving for school, the telephone rang. Isabel stopped dead in the hall.

"What if that's someone ringing to claim Blue?" she whispered.

"It won't be. Blue's—" Ella was about to say something about the Starlight Snowdogs, but stopped herself just in time. Instinctively, she knew that the Arctic magic had to be kept secret. "No one's going to claim Blue. I'm sure he's been abandoned. Why else would he have been left in a box? That'll be one of Mum's customers," she said confidently.

The school day seemed even longer than usual. Ella constantly checked the clock, wishing the hands would reach three-fifteen so she could go home to see Blue. What was he doing all on his own? Ella had left him a ball and cuddly rabbit she'd grown out of to play with, but was that enough to stop Blue from being bored?

"Can I come to yours for a bit?" asked Isabel, when it was finally home time. "I can't stay long because I'm helping Mum take Billy and Jack to the park at four."

"That'd be great!" said Ella.

Mum was up in her office when Ella and Isabel arrived home.

"Hi, Mum. It's me and Isabel," called Ella, opening the front door with her key.

"Hi, girls! I'll be out in a minute. I've just got this order to finish. Make yourselves a drink of squash and have some biscuits. There's a new packet in the tin."

"Thanks, Mum." Ella hurried to the kitchen, bursting with excitement at seeing Blue again. As she opened the door, a black and white whirlwind sped across the kitchen floor and slammed into her legs.

"Woof, woof, woof," yapped Blue, clearly delighted to see her. He jumped up and down, butting Ella with his head.

"Whoah! Steady there," said Ella, crouching down to let Blue lick her face.

"You shouldn't let him jump up like that," said Isabel sternly. "Puppies are like children. They need to be taught their manners."

Ella sighed, knowing Isabel was right. Dad had said something similar last night about letting your dog know who was in charge.

"Down," she said, pushing Blue away.

Blue cocked his head in surprise. He stared at Ella, making his blue eyes large and appealing, then jumped up at her again.

Ella fought back a giggle. "Down," she said sternly.

With a little grunt, Blue stopped jumping and sat at Ella's feet.

"Good boy," she said, patting his head.

"You might want to change that when you see what he's done to the kitchen," said Isabel.

Ella looked up and gasped. She'd been so busy saying hello to Blue that she hadn't noticed the mess. Blue's cardboard-box bed had a large hole in the middle and there was chewed cardboard everywhere. One of Daisy's skating boots had been dragged into the middle of the floor, its white lace torn to shreds, and Ella's old cuddly rabbit was now tail-less.

"Quick!" said Ella, her eyes round with fear. "Before Mum sees."

She ran into the utility room and pulled a dustpan and brush and a stiff broom from the tall cupboard.

"Give me the broom," said Isabel.

She swept the mess into one enormous pile, then stood back so Ella could use the dustpan and brush.

"I'll put this in the utility room with the other shoes," said Isabel, picking up Daisy's skating boot. "I hope she's got spare laces. This one's ruined. You're going to have to keep that utility room door shut to stop Blue getting at them."

As Ella swept the rubbish into the dustpan, Blue lunged at the brush, his long black tail with its cute white tip waggling as he attacked it.

"No!" said Ella firmly.

She pushed Blue away, ignoring the hurt look on his face. Ella's hands were sweaty with fear. If Blue didn't learn how to behave, Mum and Dad wouldn't let her keep him. That would be a disaster. In the short time Ella had known Blue she'd fallen totally in love with him. And what about the Starlight Snowdogs? How could she be their new leader without Blue?

Ella emptied the contents of the dustpan

into the bin before returning it to the cupboard. Isabel re-hung a tea towel that Blue had pulled from its rail. Ella scanned the room, making sure the kitchen was back to its usual tidy self.

"That was close!" she said, grinning at Isabel.

"What's that?" asked Ella's mum, coming into the kitchen with a stack of envelopes. "Invoices," she added, dumping them on the table.

"Nothing," said Ella hastily. "Wow, you've been busy! Would you like a drink of squash?"

"Thanks, but I need a cup of tea. Does Blue want to go out, or is he just scratching?"

Ella spun round and saw that Blue was frantically scratching at the wooden door. Then he opened his mouth and howled. Ella felt goose bumps breaking out on her arms. This was it! The Starlight Snowdogs were calling.

Ella glanced at Isabel, but she was busy pouring lemon squash into two glasses. Blue howled again, urging Ella to hurry.

"Looks like he needs the toilet," she said calmly, hoping her mum wouldn't notice her trembling hands. "I'll take him out in the garden. The biscuits are in the cupboard next to the cooker, Izzy."

"I know," said Isabel, reaching for them. "Do you want me to come with you?"

"No, thanks. It's fine, I won't be long."

Ella opened the back door and fled after Blue, who was charging down the garden towards her den. Why had she said that she wouldn't be long? What if Isabel came looking for her and discovered she was missing?

Catching up with Blue, Ella stretched out and sank her fingers into his soft fur. He lifted his head and howled loudly. Now Ella was touching him she could hear the Starlight Snowdogs howling back. This time she managed not to fall over as they raced down the garden, dodging the fleeing bantams. There was a moment of panic when Ella thought they might plough straight

through the fence, but Blue didn't hesitate.
Muscles bunching, he jumped into the air,
pulling Ella with him.

Chapter 6

Ella's breath was sucked from her as she flew upwards, her stomach flipping like a pancake as Blue went higher. As the houses and gardens shrank away, the sky darkened and the temperature plummeted. An icy wind stung Ella's cheeks, making her eyes water. Shivering, she hung on tightly to Blue, determined not to let go. But the snow-laden wind battered her and soon her fingers were too numb to hold on to anything. The wind prised them open and wrenched Blue away.

It was very dark and incredibly cold as Ella spun through the air. She was freezing and aching all over when suddenly the wind dropped. Feeling something solid beneath her, Ella looked down and saw she was flying through the air on a sled. It was pulled by Blue, his long white-tipped tail proudly arched over his back.

The night sky teemed with silvery stars. Impulsively Ella flung out her arms. The sparkling starlight seemed to fill her with a fizziness like bubbles. It was the most wonderful feeling ever. Her body tingled from the top of her head to the tip of her toes, and she longed for the sled ride to last forever.

Blue dived and Ella gripped the sled tightly as it flew down into a haze of flashing pink and green lights. The lights twirled and spun across the sky, twisting into long ribbons of green and pink that had no beginning and no end. Ella laughed, tossing back her pink-and-green-tinged hair so it spilled down her back. The lights danced on, bathing Blue and Ella in a magical mix of colourful flashes as the ground sped closer.

Ella screwed up her eyes against the wind rushing past her face. She gripped the sled tightly, bracing herself as it hit the ground and slid to a wonky halt. Ella was thrown forward, but she hung on and didn't fall off.

Blue stood proudly with his back straight, ears pricked and tail arched. After a pause, he said, "Are you getting off?"

"Sorry," said Ella hurriedly.

She clumped towards him, her legs and feet moving awkwardly in the red padded trousers and snow boots that had magically appeared with the sled. She hugged Blue, but he remained standing stiff and proud. Ella hesitated. Then, hearing panting, she let him go and stood beside him.

The Starlight Snowdogs appeared, galloping over a hump in the snow. Acer was in the lead, then Honey and Bandit, vying for second place, followed by Coda, with Inca a few paw-lengths behind. Acer slowed and stopped in front of Ella, his proud head reaching up to her waist. Ella caught her breath. She'd forgotten how large and handsome Acer was. His head was black and his face white — the fur arching like eyebrows over his deep brown eyes. His ice-white belly and legs contrasted sharply with the band of black fur that extended across his chest like a sash.

Blue fell flat on the floor with his nose resting between his front paws and Ella only just stopped herself from doing the same.

"Hello, Ella," said Acer, his low voice sending shivers up her spine. "We have a situation in town that needs your help. Get on the sled and I'll explain as we travel."

Eagerly Ella climbed back on to the sled, but Acer stopped her.

"That's where passengers ride. You're not a passenger any more. You are the leader of the Starlight Snowdogs. Go and stand at the back."

Embarrassed that she hadn't worked that out for herself, Ella went and stood on the runners at the back of the sled. Her gloved hands rested on the curved handrail. The dogs took to their harnesses in pairs, standing with their ears pricked forward and tails arched over their backs. Ella's stomach fluttered with a mix of excitement and fear. Was she really going to drive the sled by herself? She hoped she was up to it.

"That's right, hold tight to the driving bow," said Acer. "But don't forget to hold on to the gangline too."

Ella pulled herself together. If Acer thought she could drive the sled, then she could. The gangline must be the thing that looked like reins. It was awkward picking it up with her gloves. Ella fumbled around, aware that Acer and the dogs were waiting expectantly, but at last she had it in her grip.

"Say 'hike' to get us going," whispered Blue.

"Hike," said Ella, gripping the gangline.

The sled moved forward, tipping Ella against the driving bow. She pushed herself upright, her leg muscles tensing. For a moment it was enough to concentrate on her balance, but once Ella could stand without feeling like she was about to topple off the runners, she ventured a question. "Acer, where are we going?"

"To Port Nanuk," said Acer. "A polar bear has wandered into town. It happens quite a lot at this time of year. During the summer months when the sea ice has melted, the polar bears have nothing to stand on to hunt for seals. So they come inland and live in the forests. There's not much to eat and after a summer of living on berries and grass the polar bears are ravenous and eager to get back on the ice. If winter is late and the sea ice slow to freeze, some animals come into town to scavenge. They're dangerous because they're starving hungry. We must find this polar bear and herd it back out of town, as fast as we can."

Ella was speechless. She hadn't expected her first job as leader of the Starlight Snowdogs to be quite so dangerous.

"Am I going to feed it first?" she asked.

Bandit sniggered, but Acer silenced him with a low growl.

"Town people never feed polar bears," he said simply. "It encourages them to come back. Port Nanuk has a team of polar-bear wardens who carry flares and bangers to discourage the bears. Sometimes it isn't

enough to frighten them away, so then they shoot them with a sleeping dart and lock them up in polar-bear jail. Polar-bear jail is a lonely place. It's nothing but an empty pen. The bears are left on their own with fresh water, but no food, so that they're not encouraged to stay or return once they've been released."

"How long are they kept in jail?" Ella asked.

"Until winter arrives," said Acer. "Then the polar bears can take to the ice to hunt for seals."

Ella fell silent as she wondered how she was meant to show an enormous, starving polar bear the way out of town without becoming its dinner! She needed a plan, but

she didn't know where to start. The snowdogs raced on, their paws crunching softly on the snowy ground. Away to the left, Ella saw the outskirts of a forest of tall green coniferous trees. As the forest grew closer, the snowdogs turned left towards it and the sled began to tilt.

"Shift your weight," called Acer urgently.

Ella gripped the driving bow nervously, not sure what to do.

"Lean!" barked Acer.

The sled continued to tip, pitching Ella sideways. She hung on tight, snow splattering her snow glasses as the ground rushed nearer. Any minute now and the sled would capsize. Ella fought back the panic rising from her stomach and leant away from the snowy ground. Her leg muscles protested, but she stood firm, hanging on to the driving bow for all she was worth.

Several moments passed where the snowy ground seemed far too close. Ella gripped the driving bow tightly, trying to shift her weight to the right, fighting with the tilting sled that was forcing her body in the opposite direction. At last she did it. With a soft thump, the sled's runners hit the ground again. Ella hung on, her teeth jarring with the impact. The sled skidded across the snow and, without knowing what she was doing, Ella pulled on the gangline. The dogs slowed, Ella shifted her weight again until the sled stopped sliding and carried on in a straight line.

"Good work," said Acer.

Ella huffed out a sigh of relief. She wasn't sure how she'd done it, but she'd stopped the sled from overturning and got it going straight again. Realising that it was up to her to steer, Ella stopped worrying about the polar bear and concentrated on driving the Starlight Snowdogs. As they approached the forest, she realised the dogs were heading right for it at full pelt.

"Easy," said Ella, hoping she'd given the right command to slow down. She didn't fancy driving through the trees at the same break-neck speed as they'd been crossing the snowy landscape.

"Easy!"

For one scary second, Ella imagined being pulled through the forest totally out of control and crashing into a tree trunk. But the dogs had heard her and were losing speed. The rich smell of resin was overwhelming as they entered the woods, reminding Ella of her mum's bubble bath. Quickly she blanked all thoughts of home, knowing she must concentrate on steering the sled.

The forest was very dark and the sound of the panting dog team echoed eerily around. Acer kept close to the forest's edge, cutting across one corner and as the trees thinned, Ella caught a glimpse of Port Nanuk. The setting sun hung over it, painting the town a rosy red. It was a small simply-built town and the buildings all had space around them.

"Go right," said Ella automatically.

"Gee," Acer corrected her.

"Gee," said Ella, shouting the word.

The dogs turned right, and Ella only remembered to shift her weight as the sled began to tilt over. It was scary and exhilarating. Ella wished they could keep going until she'd learnt how to drive properly, but there was no time to practise now. As they neared the town, Ella realised she still didn't have a plan.

"What now?" she called to Acer.

"We find the polar bear and herd it back to the forest," said Acer, as if this was the simplest task in the world.

Ella held her breath. Polar bears looked cute and cuddly on the television, but in real life they were powerful meat-eating animals and this one was ravenously hungry. Ella's skin prickled with fear, and her stomach sunk all the way down to her snow boots at the thought of coming face to face with it.

Chapter 7

There were no roads to bring people into Port Nanuk, only a railway line. Ella drove the sled alongside the tracks, keeping a safe distance from the rails, even though she saw no trains. They followed the tracks over a flat plain of snow to the edge of the town. There, Ella found the start of a road and pulled left on the gangline.

"Haw," called Acer. "And don't forget to shift your weight."

"Haw," cried Ella, leaning as the dogs veered to the left to join the start of the road. Its surface was covered in a thick layer of packed ice, but the dogs didn't slow.

"Easy." Ella was unsure about travelling too fast on the icy road and slowed the dogs down to a jog. Thankfully the road was completely empty. There were small shops along one side of it, but everything was closed up for the night and there were no people around. It would have been deathly silent, had it not been for a loud wailing siren that made Ella's ears ache.

"What's that?" she asked, wincing. She

longed to cover her ears with her hands, but didn't dare let go of the gangline.

"Polar-bear warning," said Acer. "When the siren sounds the people of Port Nanuk stay inside until the polar bear has been caught or gone back to the forest."

The hairs on the back of Ella's neck prickled with fear and she felt queasy. The locals were safely hidden indoors. So what made her think she was up to the job of herding a dangerous animal out of town?

She stared at the backs of the huskies as they padded on, their claws tapping on the icy road. They looked so proud with their plumed tails arched high over their backs and their ears keenly pricked forward.

I'm their new leader. Of course I can do this, thought Ella, wishing she felt as confident as she sounded.

Blue and Inca were almost running to keep up with the larger dogs. It was comforting to remember that they were learners too and she wondered if they were nervous.

As Ella convinced herself that she could manage the task, she felt a magical sensation that made her insides fizz like sherbet. Ella held on to the feeling, loving that as it grew in strength she felt much braver. She could achieve anything!

"I smell a polar bear down the next street," barked Acer.

"Gee," said Ella.

Full of new confidence, she pulled right on the gangline, directing the dogs into the side street while leaning into the turn. There was a small motel on the corner of the road, its doors tightly shut. As they passed it, the dogs began to strain. A loud clattering noise startled Ella and a metal dustbin rolled into the road. The bin was badly dented, like it had been hit by a lorry. *Or attacked by a polar bear*, thought Ella, nervously eyeing the deep claw-like scratches in it.

"Easy," she called to the dogs, her voice faltering as a dark shape lumbered from the shadows. In a panic, Ella yanked on the gangline, pulling hard until the dogs stopped. Ella's mouth fell open. She could only stare in awe as an enormous polar bear casually crossed the road.

Reaching the middle, the bear stopped and sniffed the air. Sensing Ella and the dogs, it turned to face them. Ella's heart thudded painfully. She was so scared she almost stopped breathing.

Now what? How could she approach an animal that was so huge and hungry, and somehow herd it out of town?

The polar bear continued to stare at Ella and she stared back. The poor animal looked starving. It was far too thin — its ribs clearly visible through its creamy white fur. The polar bear's eyes were small and dark and it had tiny ears, but its teeth and claws were huge and lethal. Slowly lifting a colossal paw, the polar bear stepped nearer.

The fizzing feeling inside Ella was so strong she felt like she might burst. Hardly aware of what she was doing, she flicked the gangline and shouted, "Hike!"

The huskies leapt forward, running at the polar bear. "Yah!" shouted Ella, as loudly as she could. "Yah!"

Her voice exploded from deep inside her. It sounded remarkably like gunfire and made her jump with surprise. How on earth had she done that? Encouraged by her new-found talent, Ella yelled again, "Yah!"

The bear was badly startled. It spun round on all fours and loped off in the opposite direction. Ella urged the huskies forward, chasing the polar bear to the top of the street where it turned into the next road. Frantically Ella tugged on the gangline, but she'd left the turn too late and as the dogs cornered, she made things worse by forgetting to shift her weight. The dogs' paws slid on the ice and it was too much for Blue and Inca. Unused to pulling a heavy sledge, they lost their footing and were pulled round on their bottoms by Acer and Honey.

"Move," bellowed Bandit, slamming into the back of Blue.

The sled slewed sideways and tilted on one runner. Ella hung on to the driving bow. Desperately she leant the other way while pulling hard on the gangline. The sled teetered. Was it going to capsize?

For a split second, Ella thought she'd done it. But then the sled hit a lump of ice and over it went, flinging Ella into the air.

As the ground rushed towards her, she had a weird sensation of everything moving in slow motion. She was terrified she'd lose the huskies. And then what? How would she survive in this strange town with a rampaging polar bear on the loose? The fear helped her to hang on to the gangline. Instinctively Ella curled herself into a ball before she hit the ground.

Luckily she landed in a pile of snow and not on the hard ice-packed road. The sled landed beside her, narrowly missing pinning her to the ground. Everything hurt, but it was far too dangerous to stay where she was. Ella struggled up, her snow glasses askew. She quickly righted them so she could see properly. The dogs stood in a long line with their heads down, long tongues hanging out and steam rising from their heaving sides. Blue and Inca were still on their bottoms but they hurriedly stood up. Ella stared at them miserably. She wasn't a worthy leader. She was useless and a failure.

"Jak would never have crashed on an easy turn like that," said Bandit, making Ella feel even worse.

Ella wondered who this clever Jak was, but

wasn't going to give Bandit the satisfaction of asking. His comment stung her into action. She'd show Bandit how well she could drive! She knew she could do it. Why else had she been picked to lead the Starlight Snowdogs? At once Ella set about righting the sled.

"Shouldn't Blue and Inca go at the back, seeing as they're the smallest?" she asked.

"Strongest dogs go at the back, everyone knows that," said Bandit. "You should get rid of Blue and Inca. They're far too young to drive a sled."

"Bandit, that's enough!" snapped Acer. "This isn't an ordinary sled and we're not ordinary dogs." His voice softened as he addressed Ella. "That's right. Think strong.

Hurry now or we'll lose the polar bear."

The polar bear had disappeared, but further along the road a tall man dressed in a bright yellow jacket and carrying a rifle was climbing into a four-wheel drive. Ella realised he must be a warden.

Ella was determined to prove she was a good leader and beat him to the polar bear. She stood with both hands on the sled and concentrated on being strong. The muscles in her arms began to prickle. Ella pulled at the sled and to her delight it righted easily. She hopped on to the back runners, holding on to the driving bow with one hand and the gangline with the other.

"Acer," she said. "Where is the polar bear

now? Can you smell it?"

Acer threw back his head and sniffed the air. "Heading towards the bay," he replied.

"Is there a short cut so we can beat the warden?"

"It's the other way," said Acer.

It was awkward turning the sled in the road, but Ella felt a huge sense of achievement when she managed it. "Hike," she called, flicking the gangline. "Lead on, Acer. Show me where to go."

Smoothly the dogs ran forward, leaving the road and racing over a large expanse of snow. The sled skimmed effortlessly across the land and with the freezing air whipping against her face, Ella felt like she was flying. It was wonderful and made her feel braver as she urged the dogs on.

A short while later, Ella could smell the sea. In the distance was the polar bear, casually strolling towards a small collection of ugly buildings. Realising they were approaching the port and there might be people around, Ella urged the huskies on.

"Hike!" she shouted encouragingly. "Hike!"

The dogs ran faster, gaining ground on the polar bear. As they drew closer, Ella screwed up her eyes in concentration and bellowed, "Yah!"

Her voice was like a banger exploding into the frozen air and echoing from the port buildings. Ella allowed herself a small smile as

the startled polar bear shied away and loped back towards the town. Ella turned the huskies using the sled to cut it off.

"Yah!" she shouted, herding the polar bear across the snow to the side of the town. Fired up with adrenalin and a magical bubbly feeling, Ella leant over the driving bow as if that would help the snowdogs run faster.

At last the town was behind them, but Ella kept up the pace, pushing the polar bear on towards the safety of the trees. It was almost dark, but as the polar bear approached the forest Ella saw two flashes of white lurking on the outskirts. The polar bear ran straight towards them, powdery snow flying up from its enormous paws.

"Easy," called Ella, knowing the polar bear was nearly safe. She pulled on the gangline. "Easy, now. Whoah."

As the dogs stopped, Ella stared at the forest. Was that... yes, it was! Two fluffy white polar-bear cubs ventured out from the trees to meet their mum, who greeted them with a playful cuff. The cubs were so tiny they looked cute enough to cuddle, unlike their enormous mother.

"Well done," said Acer, his voice warm with approval. "On your first mission you've saved not only the mother, but also two cubs."

Ella frowned. What did Acer mean? Then it dawned on her. If the warden had captured the polar bear, he wouldn't have known about

the cubs. He'd have thrown her into polar-bear jail, leaving them alone in the woods, where they'd probably starve.

The mission hadn't been easy. Ella had been petrified, she'd crashed the sled and she'd almost felt like giving up. But if she had, the consequences would have been terrible. Suddenly Ella appreciated the greatness of her Starlight Snowdogs role.

Chapter 8

The polar bear and her cubs retreated further into the wood. Ella watched them until the last flash of their white tails melted into the darkness. The Starlight Snowdogs stood in their harness — bodies tense, tails arched over their backs, as they patiently waited.

"Free," said Ella hurriedly, remembering

she needed to give them the command to step down from the sled.

The harness magically fell away and the six dogs rolled ecstatically in the snow. Blue ran round in circles, pushing the snow into a ball with his nose, then rolling it to Ella.

"You want me to throw it?" she asked uncertainly.

"Yes," said Blue, his mouth open in a laugh.

Ella looked at Acer, who nodded.

She picked up the snowball and threw it in the air. Blue and Inca jumped together, but Blue caught it first, snapping at the snowball so it disintegrated in a cloud of white snowflakes.

"Again," said Inca, rolling her own

snowball for Ella to throw.

Coda came and sat down with his stocky body leaning against Ella's legs.

"Do you want to play too?" she asked.

"Yes please," he said shyly.

As fast as the three dogs rolled snowballs, Ella threw them. It made her laugh the way they jumped up and down, each wanting to catch the snowball first. Acer and Honey lay in the snow, nibbling at their paws to clean them. Restless Bandit paced back and forth.

"Come and play with us," Ella called to him.

Bandit's lip curled in a sneer. "Snowballs are for puppies."

Blue and Inca laughed and began a play

fight, tumbling in the snow together, but Coda looked hurt.

"I'm not a puppy," he told Ella.

"Snowballs are for everyone," said Ella firmly. "Come on, Bandit, let's see how high you can jump."

But Bandit just shook his head and walked off to sit on his own. Ella stared after him. She had the strong impression that Bandit didn't like her, but she didn't know why. Something nudged at her hand. Honey stared up at Ella, her brown eyes full of sympathy.

"Don't worry about it," she said kindly. "Bandit doesn't mean to be unkind. He's a little hot-headed, but he'll get over his disappointment."

"What disappointment?" asked Ella.

Honey hesitated, but before she could answer, Acer barked. The Starlight Snowdogs immediately lay in the snow with their noses on their paws.

"It's almost dark. We must go to our home and you must go to yours," he said.

"Where's your home?" Ella blurted out.

"Port Nanuk," said Acer.

Ella was longing to ask more questions, but Blue was already in his harness, waiting for her. Now she'd had some practice with the sled, Ella was keen to drive the snowdogs to their home, but she wasn't sure how to get back to Port Nanuk. Guessing the reason for her hesitation, Acer said, "You've worked hard today, so you must go home before we do."

Slightly disappointed, Ella climbed aboard and settled down with her back against the rail.

"Goodbye, Starlight Snowdogs," she called as Blue began to run across the snow.

"Goodbye," they called back.

Ella's stomach lurched as Blue pulled the sled up into the air. She leant over the side, waving until the dogs had disappeared and all she could see was the black night sky. It was freezing cold and Ella huddled into her coat, with her nose inside the fur-trimmed hood. A flash of green zigzagged across the sky. Ella gripped the sled, hoping for more, but the sky stayed inky black. There were no stars to light her way home. Gradually the air grew warmer and lighter, and Ella could see Blue flying in front of her.

"We're going down," he barked.

"I'm ready," Ella answered.

She sat deep in the sled, pushing her body against the back rest as they dropped through the sky.

It was the smoothest landing so far and Ella found herself standing outside her den with Blue at her feet.

"That was brilliant," she gasped, reaching down and ruffling Blue's soft black head.

"Woof," he barked.

It took a moment for Ella to adjust to being back at home on a warm September

afternoon and not in the freezing cold Arctic.

"Isabel!" she gasped, suddenly remembering her friend was round. Ella ran up the garden with Blue haring alongside her.

"Sorry, I'm back now," she said, pulling open the kitchen door and stumbling inside.

Isabel was sitting at the kitchen table with a glass of lemon and a packet of biscuits. "You've only been gone a minute," she said mildly. "Did Blue go to the toilet?"

Ella was lost for words. She must have spent several hours in the Arctic and was expecting to have to make up an excuse for her absence. It felt odd carrying on as normal after having such an amazing and scary adventure. Ella wondered what Isabel would think if she told her the truth, but deep down she knew that the Starlight Snowdogs were her secret to keep. Hers and Blue's!

"Woof," Blue thumped his tail on the ground.

"Woof," chuckled Isabel.

She leant down to stroke him. "You're so cute. I hope no one claims you, Blue. You belong here now."

"Actually," said Ella's mum, putting down her mug of tea. "I think Blue has been abandoned. Grandad Edwards emailed back. He said Blue is a malamute: a type of husky that's very good at pulling sleds. Pure-breed malamutes have brown eyes, so Blue's eyes are the wrong colour. Grandad Edwards said that's probably why you found him in a box. He'd never be a showdog that could win prizes."

"Hooray!" cheered Isabel. "You can keep Blue, Ella."

Ella reached down and buried her face in Blue's soft fur, hiding a secret smile. Now that she thought about it, she realised that all the other Starlight Snowdogs had dark brown eyes. And she guessed it was no accident that Blue's were the wrong colour.

"Blue's still on trial," said Mum, laughing. "He's here so long as he behaves himself and doesn't dig up the garden."

Isabel drank her squash, then said it was time she was off. Ella and Blue saw her to the door.

"If I had a dog lead, then Blue and I could walk some of the way home with you," said Ella wistfully.

"Blue needs his vaccinations first," said her mum, passing them in the hall on her way to her office. "I'll phone the vet later and get an appointment for Saturday. We'll go to the pet shop and get him a bed and proper dog bowls too. Those old cat bowls will be too small when he's fully grown."

Ella smothered a grin. Mum sounded as keen as she was to keep Blue. Now all she had to do was convince her dad.

When Isabel had gone, Ella carried Blue upstairs and she looked up polar bears in her huge book of animals. She was shocked to

discover that polar bears were listed as vulnerable, which meant they could become extinct if they weren't protected.

"A major threat to polar bears is the shrinking of their sea-ice habitat, due to climate change," she read to Blue, who was curled up on her bed. "Global warming is a serious problem, but everyone can help to prevent it by doing the following things…"

Quickly Ella scanned the list. "Well, Dad has a compost heap," she told Blue. "And we recycle some of our rubbish, but I bet we could recycle lots more."

The bedroom door burst open and Daisy marched in carrying her ice-skating boot with the chewed laces.

"How did this happen?" she demanded, thrusting the boot at Ella.

"Erm," Ella stuttered. "Sorry, Daisy, I didn't realise you were back from school. I was going to tell you."

"Tell me what? That Blue has eaten my skating boot?" said Daisy crossly. "I can see that already. What are you going to do about it?"

"It's not the whole boot. It's just a lace," said Ella defensively. "I thought you kept spare ones."

"That's not the point," said Daisy crossly. "I'm going skating right now. Changing a lace is going to make me late. And what if Blue had chewed the whole boot?"

"But he didn't!" said Ella indignantly.

"He might have. Naughty dog," said Daisy, thrusting the boot at a startled Blue. "Do that again and you'll be looking for a new home."

Blue scrambled up, backing away from Daisy and nearly fell off the end of the bed.

"Daisy!" squeaked Ella. "Stop it. You're frightening him."

"Good," said Daisy. "Let's hope it teaches him to leave my things alone. And what's he doing up here anyway? Mum doesn't let Spooks upstairs."

"What's wrong with you?" asked Ella. "I thought you liked Blue."

"That was before he woke me up in the

night and ate my boot," said Daisy, flouncing out of the room. "That dog's trouble and I'm telling."

Chapter 9

Mum wasn't happy about having to deal with Daisy and Ella's argument. "There's less than an hour left before I need to start making dinner and I still have lots of work to do," she grumbled.

"Katie's mum will be here soon to take me ice skating," wailed Daisy. "How am I supposed to skate with my boot like this?"

"Stop being so dramatic," said Mum. "There are spare laces in the kitchen drawer. Ella can thread it for you while you get your things together."

"I'd rather do it myself," said Daisy stiffly, hurrying out of Mum's office.

Mum rubbed her forehead.

"Most puppies chew," she said tiredly. "If you want to keep Blue out of trouble, then it might be an idea to check no one's left anything precious lying around when you're leaving him on his own. And I wouldn't leave him in the garden. Not if you want to stay on the right side of your dad."

"I'll be more careful," said Ella, relieved she was getting off so lightly.

"And Ella," said her mum, "Blue is not allowed upstairs."

"Sorry," said Ella. "I won't take him up there again."

As Ella came out of Mum's office, Spooks was walking towards the kitchen.

"Woof," said Blue and with a friendly wag of his tail he bounced towards the cat. Spooks stiffened, his whiskers standing out like the spikes of a hedgehog. He fluffed up his black fur and, arching his back, hissed a warning. Blue bounced forward, determined to say hello. Spooks spat then slashed at the puppy with a claw, missing his nose by only millimetres. Blue sneezed, jumping back in surprise, his snowflake dog tag jingling.

Ella grabbed Blue by the collar and pulled him to safety. His collar sparkled in the sunlight streaming in through the hall and the metal snowflake made her fingers fizzle. Ella shivered with delight.

"Come on, trouble," she said, pulling Blue towards the kitchen. "Let's go and work some of that energy off in the garden."

At first, Blue wanted to make friends with the bantams. Whisper, a timid bird with feathers like gold fur, was terrified of him and ran away, but Goldie, the top hen, stood her ground, pecking at Blue when he came too near. Echo and Cluck, both fluffy white birds, went and hid behind Ella's colourful caravan den.

Ella threw endless balls for Blue to chase, but she got tired long before he did. Her legs were aching, and she realised it must be from driving the sled.

"I need more practice," she told Blue, wishing he would agree and magically transport her back to the Arctic. Ella had had a taste of snowy adventures and now she wanted more.

But Blue wasn't listening. He was stalking a butterfly that was fluttering towards the tomato patch.

"Oh, no, you don't!" said Ella, heading him off before he could trample too many of the tomato plants. "Are you listening to me, Blue? You've knocked two tomatoes off! You've got to behave, especially in the garden or Dad won't let you stay."

But Blue ignored Ella and started digging a hole.

"Blue, no!"

Clapping her hands, Ella shooed him away then pushed the earth back with her foot. Luckily it hardly showed. Remembering what Mum had said, Ella knew she couldn't trust Blue in the garden on his own.

"Come and see my den," she said. "It's really cool. It used to belong to Daisy too and we painted the outside together. But Daisy's too big for dens now."

Blue cocked his head, giving Ella a quizzical look. Ella sighed. It was frustrating that they couldn't talk together like they did in the Arctic. Blue lay down in the grass and rolled on to his back, paws in the air, flashing his white tummy.

"Do you want me to rub your tummy?" asked Ella, giggling because he looked so sweet. "All right, I'll give you a rub and then I'll show you my den."

A small part of Ella hoped that if she took Blue somewhere totally private he might speak to her. Inside the old caravan, she shut the door and drew the tiny green and yellow curtains so that no one could see inside.

"How do you like your new home, then?" she asked. "Is it lonely being here without Acer and the others?"

Blue ignored Ella and began to explore the den, sniffing at bean bags, a small table and a bookcase stuffed with books, comics and drawing materials. Ella stared thoughtfully at Blue. She had to be touching Blue to hear the Starlight Snowdogs calling her to the Arctic. What if it worked the same way when she wanted to talk to him?

Ella's heart raced a little as she followed after Blue and dipped her fingers into his thick double coat. For a moment she stayed silent, enjoying the sensation as her fingers passed through the coarser outer layer of fur, then sank into the soft fluffy undercoat. Breathing slowly to calm her heartbeat she cleared her throat and said, "Do you mind living here with me, Blue?"

Tentatively Blue put a paw on the bean bag, pulling it back in surprise as the filling shifted under his weight.

"Blue?" said Ella, uncertainly. "Say something back."

Blue continued to explore the bean bag, prodding it then slowly climbing up on top.

"OK, so that's not working. Let's try something else," said Ella softly.

Her fingers curled round Blue's silver snowflake dog tag. That was more like it. Ella grinned as the collar glowed and the snowflake sparkled with a magical pulse that made her fingers tingle.

"Hello, Blue. Can you understand me now?

Are you hungry? Shall I take you in and feed you?" Ella asked.

She held her breath, willing Blue to answer. But he was busy needing the bean bag with his front paws until he'd made a comfortable hollow to lie in.

"It's not going to work, is it?" said Ella, laughing off her disappointment. After all, a few days ago she didn't even have a dog, and now she had Blue and the Starlight Snowdogs. Grinning at her amazing good fortune, Ella said, "Never mind, Blue. You're still the best dog in the world."

She pulled a book from the bookcase and, settling down next to Blue on the bean bag with her hand on his back, Ella began to read.

When Daisy came home from her ice-skating lesson she was in a much better mood and made a big fuss of Blue, who was very excited to see her.

"You're so sweet," she said, ruffling his fur and letting him lick her hand.

"Don't hype him up," said their dad, who was making a drink of tea. "Be calm with him. If we're going to keep Blue, then we'll have to sign him up for dog-training classes. We'll ask the vet on Saturday if she can recommend someone."

"Thanks, Dad," said Ella, hugging him.

"I said if." Dad used his serious voice. "Blue

still has to prove himself, Ella."

"Yuk!"

Daisy's squeals made everyone look. She pushed Blue away from her.

"That's gross!"

In his excitement, Blue had accidentally made a puddle on the kitchen floor. Quickly Ella grabbed him and moved him away from the wet spot before he made a bigger mess by trampling in it. Daisy hurriedly left the kitchen muttering that she had homework to start.

"That's what I meant about hyping him up," said Ella's dad. "Blue's your puppy, Ella; you know where the mop is."

"Thanks, everyone," moaned Ella, as her

father disappeared to the lounge with his mug of tea. With a sigh she sloshed some floor cleaner into a bucket, then filled it with hot water while she pulled on a pair of rubber gloves.

"You know, I'd rather be facing a hungry polar bear than doing this," Ella told Blue, as she cleared up the mess. She gave the floor one last mop, then carried the bucket back to the utility room.

Ella knew she couldn't afford for Blue to get into any more trouble. If Blue was sent away now she'd lose him and the Starlight Snowdogs. The Starlight Snowdogs! Ella's stomach flipped with excitement. How long would it be before they needed her again?

"Soon," whispered Ella, crossing her fingers. "Please, let it be soon."

Chapter 10

By Saturday morning, Ella was at bursting point. The Starlight Snowdogs hadn't called her and she was desperate to go back to the land of snow. Ella was glad that Blue had an early morning appointment at the vet's — partly for the distraction, and partly because once Blue had been vaccinated she'd be able to take him out for walks. It would be such fun to go to the park together and Blue would love it too. He was a lively, inquisitive puppy who needed constant entertainment to stop him getting bored.

Mr Edwards had borrowed a dog cage from someone at work. It fitted neatly into the boot of his car and gave Blue somewhere safe to ride on the drive to the vet's.

"What a gorgeous puppy," exclaimed Miss Stevens the vet when Ella lifted him up on to the examination table.

"You're a friendly little chap too!" she exclaimed when Blue licked her face as she bent down to examine him. "How old is he?"

"I don't know," said Ella. "My friend and I found him in a box in the park. Grandad says he's a malamute and that he's been abandoned."

Miss Stevens checked to see if Blue had a microchip, a small device implanted under his skin that would identify him and his owner, but he hadn't.

"I think your grandad's probably right," said Miss Stevens, shining a small torch in the puppy's ears, then checking his eyes and teeth. She ran her hands over Blue's back and felt down his legs.

"He's a healthy boy, but he could do with a bit more weight on him. Make sure he has three meals a day of good quality puppy food. I'd say he's ready for his first vaccination so I'll give that to him now. Bring him back for the

148

second one in two weeks' time and then a week after that you can take him out for walks."

Ella's face fell. "Oh," she said quietly. "I thought I was going to be able to take Blue out for a walk straight away."

Miss Stevens smiled kindly.

"It'll go very quickly. Then Blue will be ready for puppy-training classes. Ask for details at reception. There are plenty to choose from round here. In the meantime, have you got a garden and lots of nice doggie toys for Blue to play with? Malamutes need lots of exercise as they're used to being active. They're bred for pulling sleds, you know."

"I know," said Ella, quickly adding, "I've

been reading up about husky dogs on the internet."

"We're stopping off at the pet shop on the way home. We can buy some toys there," said Mr Edwards.

"Thanks, Dad," said Ella.

"That doesn't mean we'll definitely keep Blue. It depends on how he settles," he added cautiously.

"Let me know if there are any problems," said Miss Stevens, unwrapping a syringe and filling it with liquid taken from a tiny glass bottle. "A few of my clients are looking for puppies. I'm sure I can find him a good home if he's not right for you."

Ella scowled and put a protective hand on

Blue's back. No way was anyone taking Blue from her. Just let them try! Blue wagged his tail as if agreeing with her.

"Right," said Miss Stevens, advancing on Blue with the syringe. "If you could hold him tightly for me while I just..."

She grabbed at the loose skin around Blue's neck, and jabbed the needle in. Blue let out a sharp whimper, then Miss Stevens rubbed the spot she'd injected and gave him a treat from a jar behind her.

"Forgiven me already," she laughed as Blue eagerly ate the dog biscuit, then sniffed around for more. "I'll see you in two weeks, young fellow, and you can have another biscuit then."

Mr Edwards collected a leaflet on puppy-training classes, booked the second appointment and paid the receptionist for Blue's consultation.

"Can we go to the pet shop straight away?" asked Ella.

"I suppose so. This puppy's costing me a small fortune," Mr Edwards grumbled as he helped Ella load Blue back into the dog cage.

Ella grinned, hoping her dad didn't mean it. When they got to the pet shop Mr Edwards seemed to be enjoying himself and spent ages selecting the most comfortable-looking dog bed for Blue. After that, Ella chose a blue dog lead to match his sparkly blue collar and her dad added two bowls, some grooming tools, a box of doggie bags and several toys to the trolley.

"I'm not sure how we'll get all this into the car," said Dad, as they wheeled the trolley across the car park. "The dog bed will have to go across the back seats. Goodness, is that Blue making that noise? I didn't think we'd been inside the shop that long."

Ella felt her insides turn icy cold. She recognised that sound. It was the howl Blue used when the Starlight Snowdogs were calling.

"I think Blue needs the toilet," she said quickly. "Can I have the keys, Dad? I'll take him to the patch of grass round the side of the shop."

"Better take these too," said her dad, handing Ella the car keys, then reaching inside the trolley and pulling out the doggie-bag box and handing her one. "Turn the bag inside out and use it like a glove if you need to pick anything up."

"Thanks, Dad," said Ella, stuffing the bag in her pocket as she hurried over to the car.

Blue was relieved to see her, frantically scratching at the dog cage as she opened the boot to release him.

"Wait," said Ella, lifting Blue out of the cage. "It's too far to jump. You'll hurt yourself."

The moment Ella touched Blue she heard the Starlight Snowdogs howling. Shivers ran up her spine and she flushed hot with excitement. At last she was going back to the Arctic!

Ella left the keys in the boot lock of the car for her dad, then, scared that Blue might run off without her, she carried him across the car park and round the side of the building. For a small puppy Blue was surprisingly heavy, and it didn't help that he was wriggling frantically.

Gratefully Ella put Blue down on the patch of grass, still keeping hold of his collar. The silver snowflake crackled with magic as it brushed her hand. Blue took off, running alongside the building, his ears flat against his head, his plumed tail straight as a broom. Ella ran alongside him and when Blue jumped into the air she jumped too. It felt fantastic, they were flying!

Looking back, Ella caught a glimpse of her dad, tiny now, wheeling the trolley to the car, totally unaware that Ella and Blue were flying away above him. Then everything in the car park seemed to slow right down. The sky turned from sunny blue to black and the air temperature dropped to freezing. Ella's eyes watered and the cold air stung her face, but this time the flying feeling was exhilarating. When the snow-laden wind whirled towards her, Ella knew what to expect and didn't try to hang on to Blue as the wind tore him away from her. Instead she held her arms out, like bird wings, riding the

wind as snowflakes whirled round her.

After a while Ella's fingers and toes were so cold she couldn't feel them. Just when the cold was becoming unbearable the wind dropped. Ella was suddenly clothed in her warm Arctic coat and she felt the sled, pulled by Blue, solid beneath her. Her puppy seemed to be enjoying himself too, his ears were pricked and his tail curved over his back. Ella sat back, lifting her face to the starry sky and letting their magical light sparkle down on her. A wonderful feeling made her skin tingle and she felt like she wanted to ride through the sky forever.

Soon Blue headed down, flying into a swirling mass of coloured lights that came from nowhere. The lights twirled around Ella, crossing over like green, purple and pink maypole ribbons. Faster they spun, making Ella giddy. The lights stretched out across the sky, shining different shades of purple, pink and green until finally they faded away. Ella sighed, thinking it was over, but suddenly the sky lit up again with a green backdrop streaked with every colour of purple from the deepest indigo to the palest lilac.

In a brilliant flash of colour, the ground rushed up to meet Ella. Bracing herself, she gripped the sides of the sled. Blue dropped on to the snowy ground and came to a bumpy halt, standing proudly with his tail curled and his ears forward. On the horizon the sun was setting, its orange-yellow rays silhouetted by falling snow.

"Wow! That was incredible," gasped Ella.

She jumped from the sled and hugged Blue as his harness magically fell away, but he was listening to something and remained still. Ella dropped her arms and stood beside him, waiting. Then she heard it too – the panting of animals as they ran closer.

Chapter 11

The Starlight Snowdogs raced across the snowy landscape. Acer was in the lead, with Bandit a nose ahead of Honey, followed by Coda and Inca, bringing up the rear.

Blue hit the ground, belly flat, nose resting on his paws. Ella stood proudly, hands by her sides as if she was waiting to greet royalty. Acer stopped a paw's length from

Ella, then dipped his head.

"Welcome again to our snowy land," he said.

At once Acer took up his position in front of the sled as lead dog, with Honey by his side.

"We must be quick. The polar bear is back in Port Nanuk," he barked.

Eagerly the dogs paired up, ready to pull the sled. Ella's hands were sweaty with fear inside her thick gloves, but not for herself — for the polar bear and her cubs. They had to find her before the warden did. He didn't know about her cubs. And if he locked her up in polar-bear jail, he wouldn't release her until the sea ice was properly frozen, and the cubs would starve.

Ella was about to climb on the back of the sled when it occurred to her that as leader of the Starlight Snowdogs she ought to check that both the dogs and sled were fit to run. Quickly she walked down the gangline, checking each dog. In the middle of the team, Inca was standing at a strange angle to Blue. Ella stepped closer and saw that she was straddling the gangline with her hind leg. Carefully she lifted Inca's paw, untangling her so that she wouldn't trip up when the dogs moved off.

"Thanks, I didn't notice that," said Inca gratefully.

"Well done. Now you're thinking like a true leader." Acer barked his approval.

His praise warmed Ella and she strode confidently to the back of the sled and stood on the runners.

"Hike," she commanded.

Howling with excitement the dogs moved off, their paws crunching on the snow as they ran. Ella felt more in control today. As Acer told her where they needed to go she used her weight to help the dogs alter their direction. The snow was falling more heavily, covering the ground with new drifts and blanketing the trees.

After a while, through the failing light, Ella noticed the silhouette of a familiar-looking forest away to her left. The rich smell of pine filled Ella's nostrils as the sled approached it.

"Easy," she said, slowing the dogs down as they neared the trees.

Ella skilfully steered the sled between two tall trees at the entrance to the forest. Branches soared over her head, knitting together in a thick canopy. The snow was thinner here and the ground bumpy. Ella clenched her teeth as the sled jolted along. Pine needles speckling the forest floor pinged against Ella's coat, flicked up by the sled runners. She concentrated on steering the sled between trees as she cut across the corner of the woods.

At last they were through it. Ella blinked as Port Nanuk rose before her, a weak sun falling behind the buildings, painting the sky with an orange hue.

"Gee," said Ella, guiding the dogs to the right and shifting her weight to help them with the turn.

There was a long open stretch of snow in front of them with the railway line running through it.

"Mush!" cried Ella, urging the dogs to run faster across open ground.

They entered the town accompanied by the wail of a siren. Ella tensed. It was a horrible noise that made her stomach flip with nerves and set her teeth on edge. As before, the road was completely deserted. Ella wasn't surprised. If she normally lived here she'd hide away indoors, knowing there was a starving polar bear on the loose. But as the leader of the magical Starlight Snowdogs, Ella felt braver.

As the sled slid along the deserted roads, she was surprised to see other husky dogs chained up outside many of the houses.

"What are they doing outside?" she called out to Acer. "Why aren't they indoors?"

"It's the way most dogs live here," said Acer. "Not us, though. We're allowed inside."

"But what about the polar bear?" asked Ella. "Surely it isn't safe for dogs to be out all night?"

Acer didn't answer straight away. Then in a flat voice, he said, "Occasionally an unlucky dog is lost to a polar bear. But it doesn't happen as often as you'd imagine."

Ella was too shocked to reply. Suddenly she realised how little she knew about the harsh conditions that the Arctic people and animals lived in. It knocked her confidence slightly and made her consider the importance of the role she'd been given. Why had she been chosen? Did she really have special powers?

The siren was still wailing, but suddenly Ella was conscious of another noise — a low rumbling growl and the clatter of metal. Ahead was a small café, its windows dark, its door bolted.

Pushing her doubts away, Ella whispered, "Easy."

There were butterflies in her stomach as

the dogs slowed to a crawling walk. It sounded like they'd found their polar bear, but this time Ella had a plan. Remembering how she'd used her voice to herd the polar bear away from the town, Ella intended to do the same again. But could she repeat that gunshot sound when she wasn't sure how she'd made it? Ella racked her brains trying to remember exactly what she'd done.

Gradually she realised it wasn't so much what, but *how* she'd done it – last time, she hadn't stopped to think about failure. She'd simply believed that she could scare the polar bear away. So that's what she'd do this time.

Steeling herself with a deep breath, Ella opened her mouth. She made an explosive noise that almost made her cheer with delight. There was a split second of silence, followed by a surprised clatter. Ella quietly waited for the mother bear to appear, but was totally unprepared when the two cubs shot out from behind the building. They were so cute and so comical — their anxious expressions mirroring each other. Seeing Ella and her dog team, the cubs stopped running and stopped a few paws' lengths from Acer and Honey.

Ella's first thought was to scoop the cubs up and carry them back to the forest on the sled. But the polar-bear cubs weren't furry toys to be petted and cuddled. They were wild animals. They had to be dealt with carefully, and with respect. Ella hesitated, not sure if she could herd the cubs without frightening them.

The decision was snatched away from her, as suddenly the mother polar bear burst from behind the café. The giant bear placed herself between the cubs and the front of the sled, rose up on to her hind legs and gave a terrifying roar.

Ella reeled backwards, gripping the driving bow with both hands and only just stopping herself from falling off the runners. The polar bear roared again, her mouth full of vicious teeth and her outstretched paws armed with deadly claws.

Ella went weak with fear. They were trapped. The street was too narrow to turn

the Starlight Snowdogs' sled and there was no room to pass the huge polar bear. Not that Ella would have tried it with the cubs there. The mother would have attacked the moment Ella moved towards them. Hardly daring to breathe, Ella stood completely still with the snow falling softly on her. What should she do? Would Acer know? Then, all at once she had an idea.

"Starlight Snowdogs…" Ella called impulsively.

The gangline jiggled in her gloved hands as the huskies prepared for their next command. Ella closed her eyes briefly. Doubts were creeping into her mind, but she pushed them away. She could do this. But she had to concentrate.

With slow, careful movements, Ella raised her head until she was looking up at the polar bear. For a split second they eyed each other. The polar bear went to move, but Ella was quicker. Forcing every bit of air from her lungs she made a second explosive sound. The polar bear towered above her, glaring down with small black eyes. She let out a ferocious roar, then wheeling round, she dropped back on to four paws and nosed her cubs in the opposite direction.

"Hike," called Ella, urging the dogs forward. Carefully she drove them after the polar bear. The cubs scrambled along the icy road, guided by their mother as they dashed for safety. Thanks to the mournful wailing of the siren the streets were still empty. Ella guided the huskies along the roads, remembering to shift her weight when they reached a turning and calling for the huskies to go easy. Now that the polar bear was in retreat there was no need to drive the dogs so hard. Ella kept her eyes on the lumbering polar bear and her cubs, their white tails and fluffy bottoms bobbing up and down as they ran. It was thrilling to slide along the quiet roads, helping to save the polar bear and her sweet little cubs. Effortlessly Ella guided the sled down the road, keeping a safe distance behind the fleeing bear family. Ella felt amazing until, as she reached a T-junction, things started to go wrong. The polar bears

took a right turn and accidently headed back into town.

"Down here," said Acer, guiding the sled into a parallel road. "This comes out at the same place. If we're quick we can beat them and head them off."

"Hike," cried Ella encouragingly, leaning over the driving bow to try and make the dogs run faster together.

"Move it," snarled Bandit, snapping at Blue's heels. "Faster, little paws."

"Bandit," said Ella warningly. It would be disastrous if he ran into the back of Blue like he had the time before.

"Grrr," grumbled Bandit, slowing his pace to match the others.

The sled shot down the road, arriving at the end at the same time as the polar bear family. Growling angrily, the mother nosed her cubs in the opposite direction once more. It was a tight turn, but Ella skilfully steered the sled, pushing the huskies on after the bears.

"Wrong way!" barked Acer in frustration. "This road leads to the beach."

"There's not enough room to overtake and head them off," shouted Ella, conscious of the houses on either side of the narrow road. A large moon hung in the sky, lighting the way, and soon Ella could smell the sea. The houses petered out and she gasped as the road ended in a vast beach, covered with a layer of snow. The polar bears galloped on towards the dark sea, which was slushy with chunks of floating ice.

"Whoah!" shouted Ella, pulling the dogs up to stop them from running the polar bears into the half-frozen water. The mother and one of her cubs slowed immediately, but the larger cub bounded on ahead and with a flying leap, landed on a large chunk of ice floating away from the shore. The second cub stopped at the water's edge, dipping his paw in the sea and inquisitively sniffing at it.

Ella stared as the mother nudged her cub on the beach away from the ice-slushy water before trying to rescue her second cub. With long strides she ploughed through the icy water and followed the cub on to the ice. For a few moments the two bears floated together in the water, but then there was a groaning sound. A jagged line snaked across the chunk of ice, splitting it in two. The polar bear bunched her hind legs as she prepared to jump to her cub, but the ice was too thin to hold her weight. With a splash, she was catapulted into the freezing water as her cub continued to float helplessly out to sea.

Chapter 12

The cub on the beach growled bravely and ran at the sea. The mother bear hesitated, then splashed back towards him, nosing him away from the icy water. The cub kept trying to dodge round his mother, egged on by his sister's pitiful growl as she floated further from the shore.

Ella jumped from the sled. She couldn't let

the cub float out to sea without trying to save her. There were several chunks of floating ice between her and the drifting polar bear. They looked solid enough to take her weight.

"You can do it," barked Acer encouragingly.

Carefully Ella stepped out on to the first chunk of ice, holding her arms out for balance as it wobbled. Her stomach felt as unsteady as the ice. Ella swallowed, forcing herself to stay calm and concentrate. There was no room for mistakes. If she slipped and fell she could easily drown in the ice-filled sea. Sizing up the ice chunks ahead of her, she selected the most solid-looking one. *I must believe I can make it.*

And with that, Ella jumped. The ice she landed on groaned ominously so she jumped again, on to a new chunk. Ella hesitated, breathing steadily while she regained her balance.

"I can do this," she said firmly. And using the ice like stepping stones, Ella chased after the cub.

Leaping across the ice, she finally caught up with the cub, who was now only one ice chunk away. But a large expanse of water still lay between them. Surely there was no way she could cross it?

"You can," barked Acer from the beach.

Ella badly wanted to help the cub, but the gap looked too wide.

"Believe you can," Acer encouraged her.

Ella stared at the gap. "Yes, I can jump that

far," she agreed, trying to feel more certain.

The muscles in her legs felt strange, as if they were sparking with energy. The more Ella convinced herself that she could manage the jump, the more her legs tingled. Ella rocked backwards and forwards on the ice. The gap was growing wider. Was she mad? Could she really jump that far? The small grain of doubt she was feeling swelled. As the doubt grew, the sparking feeling in Ella's legs began to fizzle out.

"You can do it," barked Acer desperately.

Ella wanted to believe him so badly. I'm the leader of the Starlight Snowdogs, she reminded herself.

As Ella thought about her magical

snowdogs team, a strange sensation came over her. The feeling stole through her body, filling her with a special confidence. To succeed she must believe in the magic of the Starlight Snowdogs, and in herself. The more she thought about it, the more convinced she became that she could do it. Ella took a deep breath and before she could change her mind, she leapt from the ice and across the sea.

It was the longest jump Ella had ever made. Cold air rushed at her face and her brown hair fanned out around her. She landed awkwardly, almost falling over, but she'd done it. Here she was, nose to nose with the polar-bear cub. The cub took a startled step backwards.

"It's OK," said Ella softly. "I'm here to rescue you."

There wasn't any time to lose. The chunk of ice was still floating out to sea, and with Ella's extra weight a hair-line crack appeared on its surface. She had to act quickly. But how could she get back to shore with the polar-bear cub? Maybe she could paddle their floating iceberg like a boat. But she had nothing to paddle with except her hands.

The hair-line crack was widening. Ella doubted that the ice would stay in one piece for much longer. She would have to carry the cub back the way she'd come. But the cub looked as heavy as Ella. Could she really carry it that far? And what if it bit her? This cute, cuddly-looking cub was also a dangerous wild animal.

The ice beneath her groaned and with a sharp crack a second line ran across it. This was no time for uncertainty, Ella had to act.

"Think strong," barked Acer faintly. Glancing at the shore, Ella was surprised to see how far she'd come.

"Think strong!" she repeated, swallowing a nervous laugh. She'd have to think exceedingly strong to carry the cub that distance!

"It's all right. I won't hurt you," Ella reassured the cub as she stepped towards her. The muscles in her arms fizzed with energy. Ella wrapped them round the cub's soft coat and, thinking very strong thoughts, lifted her up. At first the cub felt so heavy Ella was only able to raise her up a centimetre from the ice. But she concentrated hard, believing in herself. Her muscles tingled more fiercely. And slowly but surely, Ella lifted the cub higher until at last she stopped noticing how heavy the cub was. Ella scanned the semi-frozen sea, working out a safe route back to the beach. First she had to make the huge leap again.

"I can do this," she said with determination.

Ella loved the magical bubbly feeling swelling inside her, making her feel like she could achieve anything. Gripping the polar-bear cub tightly, she launched herself from the ice. The polar-bear cub wriggled in panic, but Ella kept calm, holding her tightly while murmuring soothing noises.

She did it! The worst jump was over. Ella stood for a moment, remembering her route to the shore. It was like playing a crazy game of leapfrog. Ella jumped from one creaking piece of ice to another as she made her way back.

The mother polar bear was waiting for her. Ella shivered with apprehension as she landed on the beach. Carefully she put the cub down, then stepped away. Joyfully the cub flew at its mother. Ella grinned happily as they rolled together on the snowy beach. She'd done it! She'd saved the cub from drifting out to sea to drown or become a tasty snack for a killer whale. She flexed her arms, stretching out her muscles that were now burning from working so hard.

"We have to hurry. The warden's on his way and it would be nice to finish this job by ourselves," said Acer, sniffing the air.

Ella ran to the sled, hopping on to the runners. "Hike," she cried, picking up the gangline.

Ella prepared to use her special voice to get the polar bear moving, but there was no need. The polar bear had sensed trouble too. Hurriedly she nudged her cubs away from the

beach, with Ella and the Starlight Snowdogs following. And this time the polar bear headed straight back to the safety of her forest.

"We did it!" cheered Ella as the polar bears disappeared into the woods. "Well done, Starlight Snowdogs."

Blue and Inca barked enthusiastically, then quickly fell silent as Acer spoke.

"Well done to our new leader. That was quick thinking, back there on the sea ice."

Ella glowed with happiness. Being leader of the Starlight Snowdogs was the best thing that had ever happened to her. But now the drama was over, Ella noticed again how badly her muscles were aching. They felt so weak it was making her arms and legs tremble. Exhausted, she leant on the driving bow, about to give the command for the huskies to go free, but Acer spoke first. "We've worked you too hard," he said, sounding concerned. "You should rest."

"I'm fine," said Ella.

Acer shook his head. "You must rest," he said firmly and before she could protest, he turned the sled and headed back towards Port Nanuk.

Chapter 13

At first Ella tried to drive the sled, but Acer stopped and made her sit like a passenger. She wondered where they were going as they sped across the frozen landscape, lit by a huge yellow moon.

Soon they were back at Port Nanuk. Acer slowed down in front of a salmon-coloured house with a pointed roof. As he led the sled dogs round the side of the house and into a yard, Ella realised that she recognised this place. It was the house she'd passed, when the Starlight Snowdogs had given Ella her first tour of the Arctic.

"This is our home," said Acer proudly.

The back door flew open and a striking-looking Inuit lady with a weather-beaten face stepped outside. She was wearing clothes similar to the ones Ella's own grandmother wore and her long dark hair was tied back in a ponytail. She looked pleased, but surprised, to see Ella.

"Hello there. "

The lady's voice was low and friendly with a Canadian accent. Ella was normally shy about meeting new grown-ups, but she felt strangely at ease.

"My name's Saskia Tanaraq. Welcome to Port Nanuk."

"And I'm Ella Edwards." Ella pulled off her glove to shake the nut-brown hand Saskia held out to her.

"Welcome to Port Nanuk, Ella, and congratulations. The Starlight Snowdogs tell me you're doing a very good job as their new leader."

Ella stared at Saskia with growing excitement. At last, here was someone who knew about the Starlight Snowdogs! Would she answer her questions? Ella had so many, she didn't know where to start.

Saskia smiled kindly. "There's lots to take in, isn't there? You look exhausted and frozen. Come inside and rest for a bit. I'll make you a hot drink."

Ella suddenly realised how cold she was. The bottom half of her trousers were wet from the sea and a thin layer of ice had formed on them, so they crackled when she moved. She smiled at the huskies before following Saskia inside. They were lying contentedly in the yard. Bandit was missing, but Acer didn't seem concerned so Ella didn't worry either.

It was warm and cosy in the house. Ella took off her snow glasses, then peeled off her coat and hung it over the back of a kitchen chair.

"Sit down," said Saskia, filling two mugs with boiling milk from a pan on the cooker. "The siren's stopped, so I'm guessing you herded the polar bear to safety?"

"Yes," said Ella, gratefully sinking on to the chair she'd hung her coat on. "She had two cubs with her."

"A female with cubs!" exclaimed Saskia. "That's unusual. It's mostly the bold young males that come into town. The female must have been so hungry. Tell me what happened."

She put a mug of hot chocolate in front of Ella, along with a plate of home-made cookies. Ella was starving hungry too. Taking a cookie, she bit into it, then smiled at Saskia.

"It's delicious."

"My grandson made them," said Saskia proudly.

Ella privately wondered if that was the sad-looking boy she'd seen at the window. But Saskia wanted to know all about the polar bear and cubs, so Ella described how she and the Starlight Snowdogs had helped the family safely back to the forest. She was careful not to sound like she was bragging about her own role, but Saskia guessed how brave she'd been.

"It's such a relief to know that the Starlight Snowdogs are in safe hands," she said, her face crinkling into more lines as she smiled at Ella. "I was their leader for a long time, but it's definitely a job for a young person."

"Is there just one team of Starlight

Snowdogs or are there others?" asked Ella, thinking that it was a lot of work.

"Yes, there's only ever been one team."

"Why was I chosen to be their new leader?"

Saskia wrapped her hands around her mug.

"Only someone incredibly special can lead the Starlight Snowdogs," she said at last. "That special person has to believe in magic."

Modestly, Ella stared into her hot chocolate. She was proud that Saskia thought she was special, but a bit overwhelmed at the thought of living up to her new role.

"I'm still surprised it's me — I don't even live here," she said.

"That's another reason why you were chosen," Saskia explained. "You have a message to spread. For a long while, the winters have become warmer and later in arriving. Scientists blame the late winters on global warming caused by pollution. Many animals are in danger of becoming extinct because people around the world do what they want without thinking about the consequences. Being the leader of the Starlight Snowdogs isn't just about your work here. There are many ways to minimise pollution and help reduce global warming. By finding out about those ways and spreading the message where you live, you can make a huge difference."

Ella sat in silence, her head buzzing with thoughts. Saskia took a sip of her drink.

Setting down the mug, she continued. "Very few people truly believe in the power of magic. That wasn't the first time Blue had been left in a box, waiting to be found. He'd been to several other locations, but no one heard his magical howls until you came along."

Ella was surprised and pleased. "I used to get teased for believing in magic, so now I keep it a secret."

Saskia nodded. "Believing in magic isn't enough, though. You have to believe in yourself too."

Ella remembered the doubts she'd had and how she'd felt stronger when she'd fought them off. A confidence even stronger than before filled her. Being leader of the Starlight

Snowdogs was a huge challenge. But Ella Edwards was ready for it.

In a companionable silence, Ella and Saskia finished their hot chocolate, then Saskia picked up the mugs and put them by the sink.

"It's time for you to go," she said.

"Will I see you again?" asked Ella, putting on her coat.

"Definitely," said Saskia. "I'd like to help you and the Starlight Snowdogs. You're always welcome here."

Out in the yard, the dogs were lying together, except for Bandit, who appeared from round the side of the house. The dogs

jumped up and Blue gambolled over to Ella.

"Ready to go?" he asked, pushing his cold nose into her hand.

"Yes," said Ella, quickly putting on her gloves. She was feeling much better now she had rested.

"See you soon," said Saskia, standing with the other huskies as Ella and Blue pulled away on the sled.

"Bye," called Ella.

Blue raced down the middle of the road. The cold night air stung Ella's cheeks and whipped her hair across her face. Seconds later, her stomach dipped and Ella felt herself flying upwards. A flash of green illuminated the sled, then the sky turned black as tar. Ella

sank back into the seat and let Blue carry her home. It was a wonderful ride. Ella knew she would never tire of the Starlight Snowdogs' magical sled.

When at last the sled began to lose height, Ella closed her eyes tightly. Blue landed back where they'd started, round the side of the car park on a scrubby patch of grass. He sat on Ella's foot and thumped his tail, as if to say, "We're here already."

Laughing because he looked so cute, Ella lifted Blue up. "Yuk!" she said, wrinkling her nose as Blue licked her face.

Ella carried Blue to the car where her dad was squeezing the dog bed on to the back seats.

"I thought for a moment I was going to have to swap it for a smaller one," he said, shutting the car door with a grunt. "But huskies are big dogs and Blue will grow quickly... if we keep him."

Ella was about to load Blue into his dog cage. "If we keep him?" she squeaked in alarm.

Her dad hid a grin and Ella groaned. He was teasing her! Dad was far more enthusiastic about Blue than he was letting on. She was sure that if she trained Blue and taught him not to ruin the garden, there'd be no question about him staying. Before Ella shut the cage door she ran a hand over Blue, stroking his fluffy neck. Her fingers accidently brushed against the snowflake dog tag and she paused, loving the tiny sparks of energy that came from it. For a second Ella felt the chill wind of the Arctic on her face. She closed her eyes, imagining a team of husky dogs pulling a sled across the snowy landscape.

"Hurry up, Ella," said her dad, breaking into her thoughts.

Ella sighed softly as the picture in her head disappeared. But there would be plenty of other adventures soon, she was sure. Ella shut Blue into the cage then climbed into the car and pulled on her seat belt as her dad switched on the engine.

"Hike," murmured Ella.

"What's that?" asked Ella's dad. "Did you say something?"

"No," said Ella, giggling. She twisted round in her seat so she could just see the tips of Blue's triangular ears.

"Starlight Snowdog," she whispered.

"Woof!" Blue replied.

Go on another magical journey in

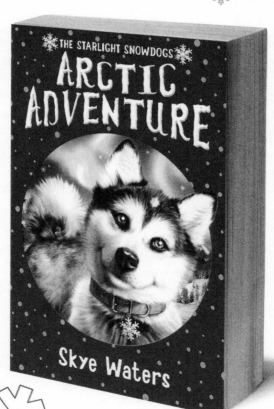